A Journey Through Everlasting Time

Harriet Clay

ISBN: **1544908768**
ISBN-13: 978-1544908762

There are two sides to every story.
There are families on either side of waring nations.
This book is dedicated to those, who despite hardships,
endeavor to do good in the darkest of times

CONTENTS

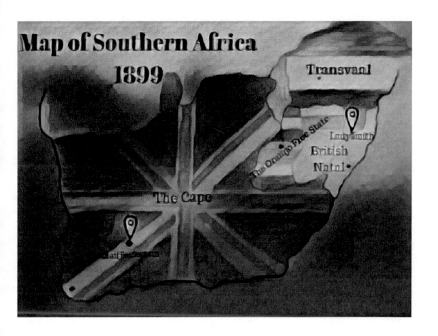

CHAPTER 1

March 1900

"Bang!" the shot rang out in the cold morning air, waking me from my deep sleep. I scrambled out of bed and ran into Stella's room. The air was thick with smoke. I could hear Jesse, crying from his cot at the foot of my bed.

"Get down Molly!" Stella yelled, "The Boers are on us!"

"We have to go now!" coughed Rudi choking on the acrid smoke as he grabbed my suitcase which had been standing, ready, at the foot of the bed for months, in anticipation of this very moment.

"You have to be brave!" Stella's eyes were bloodshot with tears. "Here, hold Jesse. Carefully now, support his little head."

We ran out of the old farm house, the red dust of the road

sticking to my sweaty forehead, towards New Train Station. I could smell the dry African bush burning, hot plumes of smoke carving up the pale blue sky. Jesse was heavy in my arms. I had never carried him this far before, and now I was going to have to look after him. Alone.

I swallowed. A large lump of bile that rose into my throat. "You have got to be brave!" Rudi said looking into my eyes that were welling with tears. "I can't leave the farm. Stella and I will come to Cape Town as soon as we can".

"I love you," I said choking up. I could hear bullets whistling through the air behind the nearby rocky koppie* and the screams of Baba Zenzile to his family as the towns people scrambled around like ants in a desperate attempt to defend themselves against this brazen attack. The British troops emerged from their tents. Panicked, Mr. Haig, the commanding officer of *The Death or Glory Boys*, came marching up the high street.

"Not now, there isn't time, come get on the train. I'll find you!" said Rudi reassuringly as he pushed Jesse and me onto the steam train. Out of the windows I could see soldiers pushing their wives onto the train; the short platform was a hive of panic as the surrounding hill side was ablaze in the eerie pale morning light. The renowned clear air of the Great Karoo was now chocked with smoke and screams.

The heavy locomotive started to pull forward, too valuable to remain at the center of this battle, the sickly smell of the steam streamed through the window as we picked up speed. I slid it closed.

And like that it was over. The warm morning sun was now

streaming through the windows and danced off my white pinafore. Just Jesse and me now. The carriage was quiet; all you could hear was the slow churning of the wheels on the metal tracks. The train lurched along pulling me deeper and deeper into my past, drawing me ever further away from the hope of getting back home.

As the heavy wheels ground to a halt at the first station I was rocked back into the present reality of my situation. It was 1900, the toddler I held in my arms, little Jesse, was my great grandfather. I was in a foreign country in a different time, I was truly lost.

I looked down as the sleeping face of my great grandfather. How was I going to escape this war and keep him safe? Most importantly, how was I going to get back to my family, back to my mom and my dad 117 years in the future! If something happened to Jesse, the future, my life, would be changed irreparably!

The conductor walked over, his heavy chain of keys chinking against his belt, showing new passengers to their seats. He stopped beside me and peered down at me through bushy eyebrows. "Where are you heading love?" he smiled kindly and sat on the bench opposite me. I shrugged and looked down at the bundle wiggling in my lap. Jesse looked up at me with his big blue eyes. His little face was so trusting, I was all he had, and I hadn't a clue what I was going to do.

I looked at the conductor who was patiently waiting for an answer. Before I could stop them a flood of tears sprang forth. "I don't know where I'm going!" I sobbed quietly into my lap. I clutched onto Jesse for some comfort but his little lip began to tremble mimicking my own expression.

"There now, the two of you," the old conductor crowed sympathetically. This war is a terrible business if the Boers would just surrender none of this would be happening.

"You don't understand; I need to get home. But if I go home who will look after Jesse? And if something happens to him there would be no point in going home, as home won't exist!" the words flew out in a nonsensical spew of panic.

The conductor's woolly face remained calm and simple. He looked at me the same way one's mother does when she thinks you're being silly; head cocked to one side with wide eyes telling you to stop, and slow down. "It's a long story," I said finally pulling myself together.

"It's a long journey," he replied kindly. "Let's try start at the beginning shall we? My name is William Coal. What's yours?"

"Molly," I replied sullenly. "My name is Molly Orpen." The train pulled away from Worcester station. The gentle rocking of the carriage swayed the exhausted babe in my arms back to sleep. I set him down carefully into the large wicker basket beside me lined with quilted blankets and two clean starched cloth nappies. William leaned forward so we could continue our discussion in whispered tones.

"So Molly," he began, "It would seem your parents have chosen to send you to Cape Town, as that is where this train is headed. Unfortunately, I don't know when it is you will be going home, back to Matjiesfontein, but don't worry I know the owner of the post office at Cape Town Central Station and I'm sure he will be able to find you a good home with some nice people to take care of you and your little brother here."

"He's not my brother! He's my great grandfather!" I protested.

"Seems you have taken shock child," William said as he got to his feet and placed his warm hand on my forehead. "You go on and take a nap now; I'll come around and wake you when we arrive in town. I'll take you to the post office myself. Terrible day you must have had. Rest up. It will all be okay." He gave my head a solid pat. The type men give when they don't want to show too much emotion, and continued on his way along the train.

I so wanted to tell him everything that had happened, but who would believe a 10-year-old girl? I closed my eyes and thought back to when it all began...

CHAPTER 2

July 2017

My Grandmother, Joan, had just passed away. It was late August and autumn was turning. Mom, Dad, Alex and I had moved into the old London house to help Grandpa settle in for a few weeks. It was three times the size of my parent's terraced house in Kent. Floorboards creaked under foot and everything seemed to be covered in a thin film of dust. It was just past breakfast time when I decided to go exploring upstairs. My grandfather, Jesse Jnr or JJ as we called him, had asked if I could bring down a few of his books from his study.

Since the renovation, moving his bedroom to the ground floor, had only been completed last week, most of his belongings were still where they had been for the last 60 years. I pushed open the old groaning chestnut door. It was heavy and not eager to move. No one ever went into this room apart from Grampa JJ. The air was thick with dust and the room smelt moldy and damp, just like his mothball infused coat. I had always wondered as a young child what was in this room, I'd visited the house often but it was not polite to go around letting yourself into rooms without permission. So, I never did.

Painted on the wall in front of me was a mural of a huge oak tree and hanging from its 'branches' were portraits of the family through the ages. It seemed to span back 5 generations!

"Wow people back then must have had an amazing life," I thought to myself. "If only they could speak, I wonder what they'd say." It was then that I heard that sweet little voice. That voice that started it all.

"They can speak".

I turned around like a shot. No one was there. I darted back to the sturdy chestnut door suspecting my little sister was snooping on me again. "Alex is that you?" I called, now standing in the doorway, looking down the long hall.

"She's not here," said the voice from behind me, inside the study! I spun around and walked into the center of the room. My eyes scanning the place for the prankster but what I saw was not a small radio or my naughty little sister, what I saw was, a fairy.

There she was, a fairy, sitting delicately on top of a pile of timeworn books. I blinked at least 5 times, the fairy remained, unmoved. I rubbed my eyes again and swallowed hard. Fairies only exist in books, I thought to myself.

"Where do you think authors got the idea from eh!" the fairy retorted.

"I did not say anything!" I gasped and clutched my hands around my mouth.

"You don't need to say anything for me to know what's in your heart," the fairy said plainly and fluttered over to the large writing desk beside me. She hopped delicately onto my shoulder and gave a sharp tug at one of my long red hairs that hung fashionably in a bob around my face.

"Ouch!" what was that for.

"A test,"

"A test for what?" I moaned rubbing my throbbing temple.

"Well you were wondering if you were dreaming, the real pain you are feeling now means you can't be asleep, or you surely would have woken up!"

I looked at the tiny creature skeptically, "Clever."

"You don't live for hundreds of years and remain stupid!" the fairy retorted rudely.

"So you're immortal then?" I asked, fascinated by the idea that I was now speaking to a tiny real life fairy!

"Don't be stupid!" the purple fairy figure fussed. "There is no such thing as being immortal. Everyone must die at some point, even fairies. I've just chosen not to die yet!"

I looked at the mini being, so small and perfect, so exactly like I expected a fairy to look. With little wings like a dragonfly, long and nimble. She was just not as nice as the stories would have you believe.

"Aren't you going to ask me why I'm here?" she said buzzing into my face.

My eyes tried to focus on the dazzling creature now sitting on the tip of my nose. She must have read my mind and I felt very embarrassed.

"You're here for me?" I asked dumbfounded trying my best to be polite.

"I've been watching you since you moved in here, I was wondering how long it would take you to notice me. You always have your face buried in that!" she pointed disdainfully towards my smart phone which was poking out of my top pocket.

"But finally," she sighed, "finally, you asked for my help, and well here we are!"

I looked around the room and moved over to the large leather chair at the writing desk and sat down, trying to steady myself.

"I don't recall asking for help at all," I said slowly beginning to wonder if I had fallen asleep in Miss Knight's class again, and this was all just a dream.

"Yes, you did ask for my help!" countered the fairy as she flew up to the top of the bookshelf. The shelves were very old; my mother had told me years ago that it was made from iron wood, a now protected species of tree that grew in Africa.

"I heard you! You wished you could travel in time!" snapped the fairy. It seemed as if she was getting rather impatient.

I smiled meekly trying to calm the angry fairy and got out of the chair and moved towards the painted wall. "I said I wondered what they would say," I pointed to the family portraits that hung on the wall in front of us.

My Mother's family grew up in South Africa and the one picture showed Grampa JJ's father, the original Jesse, standing outside the old farm house in Matjiesfontein after it had been rebuilt. Apparently, the *old* farm house was burnt down during the Boer War.

"Well you can't speak to a photograph, now can you?" said the fairy getting agitated.

"No, well, I meant figuratively." I adjusted my jeans defensively and placed my hands in my front pockets. The fairy flew onto my shoulder and nestled into my puffy sleeves. "You either do, or you don't. You can't live life in the what ifs!" she said "So again I ask, do you want to talk to them?"

"But how, you mean, like a séance? I don't think my mother would approve."

"God you really are thick!" said the fairy now drumming her fist against my forehead. "Maybe it's true what they say, too much TV rots the brain!"

"Can we just stop for a moment?" I said apologetically, "Earlier today I came in here to tidy up and get some books for my Grandpa, now I'm in a deep conversation with a *'fairy'* who in theory doesn't exist."

"I do exist, I just proved it to you, scientifically with the hair test!" she countered; her face in a snarl of frustration.

"Yes, yes," I paused losing track of my thoughts, "what I mean is this situation is not making sense. Why are you here, and why do you want to help *me*?"

"Well last night I overheard you talking about a history project you have due, and just now you wished how you could talk to these people," she said flittering towards the yellowing pictures of my family hanging off the antique wall, "so I want to help, and as I am a fairy I can grant you one wish!"

I walked away from her, leaving her sitting on the corner of one of the hanging photographs. I was thinking, skeptical that any of this was real, my whole life I had wished for magic, special powers and now here I was talking to a fairy. I turned and faced the fairy dead on. If this was a dream I might as well enjoy it!

"Really, a real wish?" I said looking into her violet coloured eyes.

"Yes"

"Anything?"

"No, there are rules. I can only grant wishes that are pure of heart."

"So no money?" My eyes flashed forward to a luxury life with all the sweets I could eat, sitting at a pool sipping something delicious out of those fancy glasses my mother only takes out for 'special guests'. The fairy frowned at me and shook her head, "That would be a selfish wish".

"What if I gave half away?" my vision adjusting to a simpler lifestyle.

"No selfish wishes!"

I looked around the room, a heartfelt wish, I mused to myself. This was, I still thought, very much a dream. How could any of this be real? "Time travel?" I said suddenly remembering my history project.

Miss Knight, my year 5 teacher, had set us the task of interviewing someone who had survived a war but then realized that most significant wars were fought over 100 years ago, and any survivors were most probably dead now. So she said we could just interview a family member about their opinions relating to war, and whether it was ever justifiable. My Dad had rudely called her a pacifist when he read the homework and had a heated debate with my Mother over the dining room table, on whether he should write a letter of complaint to the Headmaster about how teachers should not brainwash, or teach their own biased views. It ended with my mother saying if he had that much time on his hands, why were things not fixed in the house, and that the dishes seemed a better thing to get on with than writing silly letters.

I had chosen to interview Grandpa JJ whose father, my Great Grandpa, the original Jesse, had survived the Second Anglo-Boer War, to save my family another late night fight if I had chosen to interview my Dad.

"Why time travel?" said the fairy snapping me back to the present situation.

I thought quickly, even though my stomach was now rumbling at the thought of food, "So I can become as smart as you?"

The fairies face softened and beamed with a glow I had never seen before. "The pursuit of knowledge is the purest of wishes!" She gasped and looked at me proudly. "Very well, Molly Orpen, I grant you the power of time travel. Whatever you touch, as long as your heart remains pure, will become a portal, it will take you back to its origins." Her voice was stern and ominous.

"And how do I get back?" I asked quickly.

"I just told you, you now have the power of time travel, make a heartfelt pure wish to return, and you will!" With that the tiny fairy clicked her fingers and disappeared.

I blinked again. Too many mothballs, I thought to myself. I must be going loopy! I looked at the red hair that she had pulled from my head lying on the writing desk. I picked up the single strand and touched my temple from where it had been wrenched out. Maybe this wasn't all a dream? I tossed the red strand of hair aside and began to get the books and bits of paper my grandfather had sent me upstairs for in the first place.

I was nearly out the room when a small first aid kit crashed to the floor, it must have come tumbling off the bookshelf I had just been at. "Bother!" I sighed and put the heavy assortment of books I had collected for Grandpa Jesse down at the door. I walked back over to the bookshelf and picked up the rusty old kit. I studied the small box. 'M.O' was scratched into the green and red paint on the surface. "M.O, my initials", I giggled to myself. Must be for me! I opened the box with a pang of nerves bubbling inside me. I was never this nosey, but well, who would know. I pinched the two sides of the tin together and opened it. Inside, the box was crammed full of little bits of muslin cloth, a silver thimble, a large collection of sewing needles and to the side, a few lumps of lead, was it a bullet casing?

So much history in one little box I thought. I took out each item and wondered when it had last been used, by whom, and why. I held the bullet casing in the palm of my hand. What an odd thing to keep, I thought studying it.

There was an old handkerchief wrapped up neatly in the corner of the tin. I unwrapped it. There was beautiful embroidery of a daffodil on the right hand latticed edge. My favourite flower! In the middle of the soft linen cloth was a large lump of lead all distorted and pitted. What a strange thing to wrap up! I wish I knew what it was and why my grandfather kept it.

The thought had barely had time to settle in my brain when suddenly a pillar of light shot up from inside the tin. It grew bigger and bigger and within seconds I was being sucked into it! Soon I was enveloped in the glow I slammed my eyes shut to shield myself from the blinding luminosity which felt blisteringly warm against my face. After a minute

I slowly tried to open my eyes, this time squinting, the light was bright and warm, I could make out a few details. The air was warm too, hot, like when you take something out of the oven. A dry heat. There was a smell of sweet grass and dry earth. I could hear a soft cooing noise of a bird, a turtle dove nestled down in a willowy tall thorn tree. As I slowly adjusted to my surroundings, I realized where I was, I was standing outside the old homestead in the Karoo. The same building I had seen in the photograph that was hanging on the wall in grandpa JJ's study.

CHAPTER 3

October 1899

I stood dumbfounded, was this real? I opened my hand and looked at the first aid kit I had been holding. It was just the same, but my initials M.O were not scratched onto the surface. I was now starting to feel sick. I opened the tin and the shell casing, lump of lead, and pretty embodied hanky were all gone.

"Welcome to 1899!" came a familiar voice from behind me.

I shot around and just like before I saw that dammed fairy.

"This is not real!" I shouted out, "Wake up Molly, WAKE UP!" I slapped my face and pinched my arm.

The fairy grimaced, "That will leave a bruise you know."

"Go away!" I snapped. "This is all a big mistake, this is all a dream, a NIGHTMARE in fact."

The fairy flew over and roughly plucked two hairs from my head. "OWWCH!" I yelped and slapped the fairy off my shoulder. "Would you PLEASE, stop that!"

"Just proving a point," the fairy retorted.

"That this is not a dream?" I said meanly. "That this is... that this is... that this is NOT a dream!" The sudden dawning of where I was and what had happened were setting in. I looked at the farm house, surrounded by red earth and flower beds of mother in laws tongue, a spikey hardy plant, surrounded the simple dwelling.

"What have you done?" I said angrily as I gripped the fairy in my hands and angrily shook her.

"I granted you your wish!" she spat out angrily.

"My wish, my wish? I didn't wish to come to 1899!"

"Yes you did, you said: 'I wish I knew why my grandfather kept it'."

"Kept what?" I barked.

"The first aid kit, you forgetful, ungrateful madam! The one you have in your hand!"

"Yes ,well I was wondering about the bullet and the shell casing but it's not here anymore is it, so I can't ask him, can I!"

"Of course it's not there. It's not there because the reason why, has not happened yet. In fact, you can't even ask your grandfather as your great grandfather was only born 8 months ago, so even if you wanted to ask him, he wouldn't be able to tell you!"

"So then why am I here? If I can't ask and find out?"

"I find interaction, immersion, the best way to learn!" the fairy smiled. You wanted the gift of time travel so here you are, back in time!"

I looked around me; the tin farmhouse, built from sheets of painted corrugated iron, shimmered in the heat. To my left was a dusty rocky outcrop covered in aloes. To my right a grubby high street with hand painted signs to Logan's Hotel.

"Where do I go? How do I? I mean look at me!" tears were filling my eyes as I looked down, my trendy clothes transformed into a hideous itchy beige frock. The fairy laughed.

"I will admit; you do look astonishingly odd!" She fluttered over and sat on my shoulder.

"I wish to go back home," I said snuffling, mopping my forehead covered in sweat from the unrelenting sun.

"That's a selfish wish," snapped the fairy.

"What? How can it be selfish, if I wished myself here, I should be able to wish myself back!"

"Your wish to come here was pure of heart, you wanted to

learn, your wish to go back is selfish because now you are afraid!"

I could feel the hot sun burning my pale fair skin. "But I don't know anything about this place! I can't just walk into the old farm house and just act like everything is normal! Hi I'm your great, great, great granddaughter. I was brought here by a fairy. That will go down really well with the Victorians!" I snapped sarcastically. "They'll burn me! They will think I'm a witch!"

I was getting hysterical. The heat was beginning to suffocate me, my red hair simmered in the hot African sun and my cheeks were inflamed with a mixture of rage and utter panic.

"This is not Salem, Molly!" said the fairy rather matter-of-factly.

"Although I wouldn't recommend telling people you're from the future. They will probably put you in the mental hospital. Best to just blend in!"

And with that she was gone.

I stood in front of the farm house pinching my arm again and again desperately trying to wake up from this endless nightmare.

"Oi Sissy! Is jy okay?" came a loud voice. A large shirtless man who was working in the dry garden began walking towards me. He had toffee coloured skin like melted caramel. He was strong and well built. "Sissy, kan ek jou help?" The sun was baking down and I could feel the heat of the earth beneath my thin leather shoes.

21

"I… I'm lost" I said as the man got closer, "Praat jy Afrikaans?" he asked gently. Instinctively, I shook my head not understanding what he was saying. "Come with me," he said hesitantly, you could tell speaking English was just as much of a challenge for him as understanding Afrikaans was for me. My Mother, being South African, used to speak to us in Afrikaans when we were little, but no one spoke Afrikaans in England and, well, I'd forgotten most of what my mom had taught me.

I followed the man towards the front of the house. He stopped about two meters from the front door. "Ek kannie in gaan nie."

"You can't go in?" I repeated for clarification. He nodded, a more somber expression flashed across his face, one of wanting and hope.

"Hulle is tuis. Klop net." He began walking back toward the shade of a large fruit tree where he had been working.

What was I going to say? How was I going to get home? I felt a sudden wave take over my whole body. I went cold, then hot. Then everything went dark.

I awoke to find myself inside a small room with a jug of water beside me. I pinched myself again. No luck. I was stuck in 1899! I looked around, sitting up in bed. The metal springs creaked loudly and I heard someone moving outside the door. There was a soft knock and a short black lady peeked around the corner of the door. She was dressed in a simple uniform covered by a white apron. She smiled and brought a small plate of what looked like cake towards me. "Dis melktert," she said holding the plate, thrusting it forward while doing a brief curtsey. "You fainted, here eat,"

"Thank you." I said hesitantly as I took the plate from her. She had a loving smile and grinned at me. "Jy moet eet Sissy," she said nodding towards the untouched plate in my hands.

The 'melktert' was like no other cake I'd ever seen before. For starters, it wasn't really like cake at all. It was like a white jelly, like a custard that had set over a base of finely crushed crackers.

"Dis lekker, proer!" said the friendly face. I shrugged not understanding. "It is nice," she tried again.

"Ek is Molly," I said, suddenly feeling very rude as I had not introduced myself, and was trying my best to remember any sentences of Afrikaans my mother had taught me when I was little.

"I am Molly" I said again, "I'm from London"

"I am Mary" said Mary, "Ek werk heir".

"You work here?"

She nodded.

I smiled and patted the bed I was propped up in, beckoning her to sit with me, but her smile faded and she shook her head. She stood like a sentry at the door, perfectly poised watching me eat. I felt awkward. I was not used to this divide, I had never had a maid in London, I wasn't sure of the protocol. I felt like a spoilt chick in a nest eating while she had to stand watching me, the hot sun shining in the window, she must have been exhausted. I smiled meekly and tried to get out of bed. The awkward tension only made worse as Mary curtsied when I stood up.

"They are downstairs in the library room," she said slowly, "Madam has said you can borrow one of her old dresses," she pointed to a light blue dress that hung over the cupboard door. The fabric was worn and soft and the blue colour had been leeched out by the merciless sun.

"Thank you," I said still in a daze as to what my story would be. I was always a good liar at school, I had the best excuses for when my homework was missing, but this was different. I was 117 years in the past. I couldn't speak the language how was I going to fib my way out of this? The truth wasn't an option.

I took the dress off the hanger and spread it out on the bed, Mary stepped towards me. I looked at her confused. "I will help you Miss Molly," she said kindly as she turned me around and began unbuttoning my hideous beige dress which was covered in red sand and spotted with blood. I must have hit my head when I passed out.

I reached around suddenly, very embarrassed, "No, no, it's fine I can do it."

She stood back, stung by my words.

"I'm just used to doing it myself," I added quickly. Her faced softened again.

"You will need help with the buttons," she gestured towards the blue dress. There were about 20 small buttons running down the length of the back."

"I see," I said now understanding why maids would need to help with such a personal thing.

"Turn around."

I did as I was instructed. Mary's dark hands were rough and chapped. They were her tools. She was most efficient, and I was dressed and ready in half the time. "Thank you," I said smiling at her. She curtsied again and gave a nod.

"You can go down stairs now," she gestured towards the door. It had a small round brass knob which I turned and ventured down the wooden hallway. The floorboards creaked and there was a loud hissing and clicking of insects outside. I looked out of the top floor window on the landing.

"What is that sound?" I turned and asked Mary. I had never heard anything like it! I was used to the sound of traffic, of cars racing past, alarms blaring at all hours.

"It's the..." she paused "Ibhungane, the, the beetles!"

"Like crickets?"

"She nodded".

I walked nervously down the staircase lined with a red carpet. I could make out some faint voices from the room below.

"Go on they have been expecting you for months!" Mary said hurrying my nervous feet down the stairs.

"What? How did they know I was coming?"

"You're the orphan from Cape Town aren't you?" Mary

asked looking into my frightened eyes. "You're here to help around the hotel? Madam was worried you had been abducted during the attacks as you're two weeks late, but no matter, you're here now!"

"Yes", I said uneasily, "I guess, yes, I'm here now."

I continued down the stairs, it would seem I would have to slip into this new role and pretend to be this, well, orphan, until she arrived. Thankfully she never did.

"Rudolf! Rudolf! She is awake!"

I looked to the foot of the staircase where the most elegant of ladies was waiting for me her arms out stretched beckoning me towards her. Just then, two bushy heads popped around of the library door and walked out towards the foot of the stairs. The men were dressed in Khaki coloured tunics, shorts and long socks with big brown boots laced up to the ankle. A stark difference to the lady; a pillar of white lace and delicately embroidered finery.

"You look much better child" she said as I got closer.

I smiled nervously.

"We have been expecting you for some weeks now!" Poor Mr. Logan and his wife have been run off their feet!" She gestured towards a large man with a full bushy mustache.

"Hello young las!" he said as he stretched out his tanned arm to shake my hand. He had a thick Scottish accent and shook my arm firmly. "I'm Molly Orpen," I said without thinking. The second gentleman smiled and came forward. "Molly, you will be staying with us! I'm Rudolf Schutte,

James can't fit you into the hotel now that it's becoming more of a hospital than a spa." He slapped the mustached Mr. Logan solidly on the back.

"You can get settled today and I'll see you bright and early at the hotel tomorrow morning to go over what work you will be doing. Mostly clearing the tables and serving breakfast, you will be under the care of Nurse Katie who is due to arrive any day now," Mr. Logan said with a grin. He gave a nod to Rudolf and opened the front door. A blast of hot dry air swarmed in and I felt myself go faint again. "Easy now, you will need to get used to this Karoo heat if you are going to be of any use to me!" he said jokingly and took his leave strolling up the stoned garden path way, his feet crunching the gravel as he walked.

"Well that's settled then," said the elegant lady as she closed the front door. Mary was standing at the top of the landing with perfect poise, but gave me a reassuring smile as I followed my hostess into the library. She walked over to a beautiful couch set and motioned that I should sit. The fabric was flocked velvet and had pink and gold ridges which felt like the nose of a kitten to the touch.

"So tell me a little bit about yourself," she said, pouring a tall glass of lemonade, from the drink stand beside her. The beads of condensation ran down the glass. I licked my lips. The 'melktert' had left a slimy texture in my mouth and I wasn't doing very well in the heat. I sat down beside her as commanded.

"Well what would you like to know?" I offered as vague a reply not knowing what I should or shouldn't say.

Thankfully she was the one who broke the ice. "I'm Stella," she said softening. "I help Mrs. Logan at the bottling works at the end of the road. My husband who you met just now, Rudi, he helps Mr. Logan with, well, everything. This might be a small town, but it's been growing! Every day we see new faces flocking to the hotel. Just a few years ago we had Randolf Churchill stay, but now, with this war afoot, we need a few more skilled hands."

She looked down at my lap examining my soft pink hands.

"Those haven't seen a lot of work have they?" she said remarking at how unblemished my feeble paws were.

She was right. I never helped my mom at home, I'd just come home from school kick off my shoes and watch the telly. The best my poor mother could hope for was getting me upstairs to do my homework. That rarely happened either. The only thing I relished in doing and put any effort into was plotting against my little sister Alex.

I folded my arms defensively. "No matter, we shall soon put you to work. We all work here, no one is too good for it." She waved Mary over to pour me a glass of lemonade.

CHAPTER 4

November 1899

I soon slotted into my role as a dog's-body, running small errands that required a level of education Mary was deprived of. She could not read or write. She was kept busy with chores at the house. The washing for example took her at least 3 hours. She would soak Rudi's sweat stained shirts in a large metal bath overnight and use a lye soap made from a mixture of boiled animal fat and lye. (Lye made from water run through ashes from a wood fire.) She called it her black soap, due to its colour. I was disgusted to find that the chamber pots we used at night were emptied into a barrel behind the house and our urine was what the shirts were soaked in!

The only flushing toilets, a very recent invention, were to be found at Mr. Logan's house, and I was yet to receive an invitation to see it.

I was surprised by the separation of classes. Growing up in England I knew I was no royal, but I went to private school and Mom and Dad had tried to teach me everything they knew. I fitted in; I could be who I wanted to be. But here in this small town, international guests were revered like Gods, and army generals demanded respect. Everyone knew their roles and worked within them. There was no place for a surly teenager and if you didn't work, you didn't eat.

None of what I had learnt at school was at all helpful now. My chores were based on my gender and as a girl I was expected to clean, sew, iron and delight men with witty comments, but never speak my mind. Even though I was 10, I was treated as an adult, most children were apprenticed at the age of 8 to learn a skill and begin work. Schools it would seem were only for boys and the elite. And I was definitely not elite, or a boy.

To make matters worse, I did not know how to clean properly. There were no vacuum cleaners, carpets had to be hung outside and beaten with a large broom handle. There were no clothing stores! If I needed a new dress I had to order material from a catalogue from the post office and make it myself! I had never learnt how to sew, so I wore the only two dresses I had. The hideous beige one the fairy had left me in on my first day, and the faded blue one Stella had leant me. Although looking at the state of it, I was sure she would not be asking for it back.

The town consisted of just one main road. One side of the road was used as a parade ground for the military and sometimes ox wagons parked there. And just behind it was the train station. The other side of the dusty street was lined with the necessities; a farmstall, the births and deaths registration office, the post office, a pub and most importantly, the town's crowning jewel, The Logan's Hotel.

Mind you there was no parking for cars! The first car had only arrived two years ago, a Benz Velo, transported by train and displayed to Paul Kruger (The Prime Minster of the Transvaal) in 1897.

I must have seemed to be the most useless person in the small town. It had been three months since I had 'wished' myself into this nightmare and I had given up any hope of finding that wretched fairy and wishing my way back to my family.

Poor Mary had all but given up on trying to teach me how to cook, and after an incident with a puff adder in the garden, Baba Zenzile had not taken me out tracking for lost sheep since. It was clear that the only thing I was remotely good at was welcoming guests to the hotel and helping Chef set the tables for lunches and dinners. And that's how I came to work in Mr. Logan's hotel.

It was on a typically hot day when I was working in the reception at the Hotel, when I met my first friend. She was 17 years old and had long brown hair. The type that hung in thick effortless locks down her back. She had a petite frame and walked into the lobby as if she owned the entire town.

"Hello," she said self-importantly looking down at me, seated behind a desk filing away papers for Mr. Logan. He had just ordered electric street lights and the amount of admin, without having emails or fax machines, meant I was engaged, daily, in a never-ending battle with the accounts cabinet.

"Are you going to help me, or do I need to find someone who can?" she smiled knowing her thinly veiled threat was enough to make anyone jump to attention. The thought of another stern word about my organization, or lack thereof, from Mr. Logan was enough to make my blood run cold.

"So Sorry, I didn't quiet see you there from behind these papers," I said jumping up and promptly knocking my mornings work off the table. She smiled at my misfortune.

"I'm here to see General Haig, I've been sent by *Sister* Nellie Gould".

Her accent was strange, Australian perhaps.

"O you don't look like a nun," I blurted out in my teenage ignorant way.

"That's because I'm not a nun," she seemed pleased at that thought, and smiled brilliantly as if she was about to do something wicked, "I'm a nurse I've been sent here to work with Dr …" she paused and pursed her lips "You know I've quite forgotten his name."

I had been confused by the word *Sister*, as we had just as many nuns about the place praying for people, as we did nurses attending the wounded.

"The general is out on patrol with the troops, Maam. I could seat you in the lunch room, or get you checked in perhaps?"

I began ruffling through the papers on the desk looking for

the guest book. The hotel was in a state of disarray since the troops had taken over. It was now, no longer, a sought-after spa sanctuary in the middle of the Karoo. Mr. Logan had allowed his hotel, and indeed the town, to become the British military headquarters for the duration of the war. The lush guest rooms were now stripped back and transformed into hospital wards. The sounds of men moaning and writhing in agony haunted the corridors. Their wounds varying from gun shots bravely taken in battle, to snake bites accidently incurred from going to the long drop at night without a lamp.

At night, it was so dark, you couldn't see your hand in front of your face. It never got this dark in England, there was always some form of light, the glow from the fridge the red lights from the microwave, the street lights glowing constantly.

But now, when night came it was just a kerosene lamp and the stars. The moon, when full was dazzling. There was no comparison between it and the smoggy London skyline I had grown up with. London, home, my family were becoming a distant memory.

"So are you going to help me or not?"

I was snapped out of my day dream. I must have looked miserable with my thoughts of home written in tears in my eyes as her face softened unexpectedly.

"My name is Katie, why don't you join me for lunch, it must be about that time," she looked at the mess of papers on the floor, "You can finish with that lot afterwards." Her smile was warm and I felt at once at ease. I grinned back at her as bravely as I could and took her through to the dining room.

The tables had been set inelegantly, by me, for the lunch service. The warrant officers and generals would eat inside the hotel while the rest of the troops were fed in the large tarpaulin tent across on the other side of the railway line. Katie looked around at the butter yellow table clothes and walked delicately over the wooden floor towards the door that opened out onto the courtyard.

There was a large peppercorn tree in the center, its branches hung delicately like a desert willow, its heady scent filled the air. "I think this table will do nicely," she said as she placed a cushion on the wrought iron chair underneath the tree.

"I'll go and get the menu for you Maam," I smiled enraptured by her simple elegance and beauty.

"Katie, please, call me Katie, or Nurse Katie if you must be so formal," she corrected. "And tell the cook I'll have the soup, I hear it's rather famous," she winked as I disappeared inside the cool shade of the hotel. Katie had obviously heard stories about the cook's soup. A few years ago, visitors would frequently use the hotel as a half way stop for lunch while the train was loaded with more water. (Every locomotive needed 250 000 litres of water to cross the Karoo!) Cook would charge guests upfront for the lunch-time-special, a three-course meal, but he would serve the first course, the soup of the day, so hot that by the time the conductors whistle blew, signaling the train was ready to depart again, all the lunch time guests would have to make a run for the train, never eating the main course or dessert! This proved an enterprising, yet dishonest business and Mr.

Logan put a stop to it when rumours about the hot soup reached him. He decided instead to open a farmstall near the platform and sell his famous lemonade, ginger ale and soda water to the transient visitors instead. Stella my host, my great great grandmother, helped Mrs. Logan at the bottling works and would bring home a case of soda water each week which she would use to dilute her nightly tipple.

I ran into the kitchen to alert Chef that we had a guest for lunch.

"Vagrant or military?" Chef asked in his no-nonsense tone.

"Neither," I replied, "She is a nurse. Here to help the Doctor upstairs."

"That would be nurse Katie then," Chef grinned, he always knew everything! He was the town gossip always chatting to the cleaners for snippets of news about the guests, sometimes he would even pay them to snoop through their belongings! He had a bad habit of hovering about the table when serving fancy guests, just long enough to eavesdrop on their conversation.

"Do you know her?" I asked.

"Know her, no. Know of her, yes! Rumour has it she is quiet a looker! Meant to arrive months ago, wonder what kept her? She best keep herself hidden from these military men mind!"

"Don't be rude!" I gawped at the way Chef was holding up two fruits lasciviously in his course hands.

I took out a plate of grapes and cheese to Katie in the

courtyard while chef heated up some soup.

Baba Zinzele was sweeping the flagstone stoep* clear of the red earth that blew in from the dry desert. He smiled at us, two young girls in the middle of nowhere, shaded under the peppercorn tree.

"So what kept you so long?" I probed.

"Excuse me?" Katie replied astonished at how forward I was being. It would seem that my manners still had much adjusting to do to fit into polite company in the late 19th century.

"Sorry," I fumbled my words. How was I supposed to explain that I had just been gossiping about her, my newest friend, in the kitchen?

"I meant only, well Mr. Logan was expecting you a month back, and you're here now, so I was just enquiring as to what might have delayed you…"

Her face softened into a dream like smile. "Well if you must know it was because of a boy". Her smile broadened and her eyes glinted as she continued. "He is a soldier turned journalist, come here all the way from England to write about the war for The Morning Post!"

I blushed as her face beamed when she spoke of him.

"He was such a gentleman, not like those bludgers back home!"

"Where is home?" I enquired not wanting to make any more

assumptions.

"Australia," I'm surprised you needed to ask, everyone has been remarking on my accent since the boat docked in this god-forsaken country".

She looked around and scoffed at Baba Zinzele as he worked hard in the unrelenting heat. "No point in doing that," She shouted in his direction, "it will be covered in dust again tomorrow," she waved her arm dismissively. Baba Zinzelle came over, and stopped 3 feet from the table. I had learned that he wasn't allowed any closer than that. Not just because he was black, but because he was a man and it was customary for men to keep their distance from young women, unescorted.

It had taken me a while to get used to the differences between how the British and the Boers treated people of colour. White supremacy over blacks would be maintained in South Africa until their first democratic election in 1994, when my mother lived in the country as a young girl. But that was 95 years in the future; I was still trapped in the past.

"Where are you from?" asked Katie examining my fair skin and red hair with a critical eye.

"It's complicated," I replied. I couldn't tell her I was from the year 2017, lived in another country, England, but was now in the middle of the Great Karoo desert during the Anglo Boer war.

"Let's just say I'm from England," I said smiling as Chef came out of the kitchen with two large bowls of soup.

"She's an orphan mind," said Chef walking over defensively, as he placed the simmering soup on the table in front of Katie.

"O, I'm so sorry," she remarked, "didn't think," she took the large solid silver spoons off Chef and gave a sheepish smile.

He beamed. He now knew he had the upper hand.

"I'll be where I always am if you need anything else." He winked at Katie.

"Don't mind him," I chimed in as I blew on a spoonful of soup.

Katie smiled but looked, changed, somewhat vulnerable.

The cicada beetles hissed in the afternoon heat. The courtyard was suspended in a haze of emotion. "Tell me more about this reporter then," I said breaking the awkward silence. Well, his name is Winston she said.

Late November 1899

Katie and I became fast friends after our first day together. I showed her around town and took her over to my great great grandparent's farm house to visit my great grandfather, Jesse who at the time was just learning to crawl.

She didn't need to know that I was from the future. She dint care how I came to be in this small town, to her I was just like her, displaced in a foreign land because of war.

We sat on the front stoep* drinking Logan's famous lemonade while Jesse clambered over the hand knitted blanket we had laid out on the cool slate floor for him. The weather was glorious. The heat no longer felt as oppressive as it had been when I first arrived. I had become used to the dry air and the desert climate. In the evenings a light breeze would pick up and as darkness fell the whistle of it over the zinc roof lulled me to sleep.

When I wasn't working at the hotel I would help Mary in the kitchen. The staple meat was Karoo lamb which we would have for dinner in all forms. Lamb leg, lamb chops, lamb cheeks! Preparing it was something to get used to at first. The meat wasn't prepackaged from the supermarket as I was used to. Here it came tied up in brown paper delivered once a week from Farmer John who would bring the meat to the back door, never to the front. There were strict rules about who could use the front door. Mary and Baba Zinzile were never allowed to use the front door, unless Mary was cleaning the threshold. Nothing we used was ever wasted even the bones of the lamb were boiled once for soup, then ground into powder to use in the garden. The hooves could be boiled down and used in Mary's jelly, but she said she preferred ox hooves as the lamb had such a strong flavor it would ruin the subtle taste of the jellied fruits.

Mr. Logan had large orchards of fruit trees growing just outside town, propagated by his well of water, the fruit trees thrived in the heat of the desert.

Katie and I for a brief spell were so happy, it was almost as if the country was not at war and we were merely extras on a strange film set, playing our parts happily.

Jesse smiled at me as he tugged at my red curls and bounced up and down on my knee. I was happy, but it was not to last.

CHAPTER 5

December 1899

It was now mid-December, Mr. Logan had returned from his travels and the war was gaining momentum. The mood in the town was somber; it had been a disastrous week for the British Army. They had suffered three devastating defeats by the Boers at the battles of Stormberg, Colenso and Magersfontein. Overall close to 3000 men had been killed, wounded and or captured.

Most poignantly of all, Mr. Logan's friend, General Wauchope, had tragically lost his life in battle when The Highland Brigade was ordered to make an attack at dawn.

Due to several blundering errors the force was spotted before they were equipped to launch their attack, the enemy positions had not been properly located; which lead to the troop coming under heavy fire. Sadly, Wauchope was killed in the opening minutes of the conflict.

To further add to the drama, Wauchope had been buried shortly after the battle with full military honours near to where he had died. However, Mr. Logan had been instructed by his friend's, now widow, that she wanted her husband buried in Matjiesfontein. It would seem the heartbroken old bat had no clue as to how far apart the two locations were, and how much trouble it was to transport a dead body over miles of wild terrain; fighting off hyenas at night, sniffing the acrid flesh which rapidly putrefied in the African sun.

The heat was ferocious as the sun beat down on the few survivors who had marched back to town lead by Captain Rennie and Mr Robertson, the Highland Brigade's chaplain. Wauchope's body was latched inside a most humble coffin, to the outside of a wagon carrying wounded soldiers who had been transferred from the British camp at Modder River to be treated here in Matjiesfontein.

A day later the whole town gathered for a grand second funeral. I glanced around the sea of faces, the soldier's burnt skin red in the remorseless sun. Their faces were hollow; haunted by the battle they were lucky to have survived. The Hotel was at bursting point, the wounded filling every available space. Poor Katie was run off her feet.

I looked for her in the crowd gathered in the small cemetery. I saw her stood next to Edgar Wallace, he worked some days in the post office as a war correspondent for Reuters.

Katie looked distressed and Edgar looked uneasy, as if what they had just been discussing should rather have been kept for a more private audience. Katie's eyes glazed over with tears. Just then she looked up and caught me staring at her. She grimaced, turned and left. Edgar fanned his hand over his brow as Mr. Logan glared at him over the disruption. I wanted to chase after her and find out what was wrong, but I was rooted to the spot, if I moved now it would be terribly disrespectful.

A firing party from the Duke of Edinburgh's Own Volunteer Rifles (the Dukes), commanded by Major Woodhead, fired the final salute. A huge memorial plaque was to be erected in the coming months once the stone masons had completed the engravings.

The silence had been broken and we were dismissed. The family and friends of General Wauchope made their way back for a late tea at Mr. Logan's home.

"Hello there Miss Orpen, fancy a lift into town?"

It was a long walk back, close on 10 km's, and I was happy to be offered a lift on the back of Edgar's horse.

"Yes please".

I clambered up most inelegantly. I was not used to getting onto horses, not to mention a war horse this size! Moments like this made me long for the back seat of my mother's Volvo with the air-conditioning on full blast!

"What were you discussing with Katie?" I asked nosily. Katie and I had become very close over the last month and I was bound to find out, whether Edgar decided to tell me, or not.

"Well, its personal," he started, adjusting himself in the saddle as we ambled along the dusty road. The horse's hooves clopped along the mix of quarts and sand, and the desert wind was a welcome relief as it blew across the vast expanse of land before us.

"Shall I ask Chef then?" I teased.

"No! Heavens! If he gets word of this the whole camp will be up in arms, not to mention Katie might lose everything!"

"How so?" I leant back into his chest, his body shielding me from the sun.

"Do you remember when she came to work here she was late in arriving for her post?"

"Yes, she mentioned it was because of a journalist she had met in the Cape."

"Well," he said conspiratorially, "Do you know who that man is?"

"She said his name was, Wesley or something".

"Not Wesley, but Winston!"

"Yes, that's it!" I said, suddenly remembering the conversation we had had under the large peppercorn tree on the day she came to town. "So, what's so special about this lad then," I enquired.

"Well, post came in today for Katie. With all the war correspondence, I mistakenly opened her letter. It was from him!"

"Well don't hold back! What did it say?" I pressed, loving the drama and mystery behind something as simple as a letter.

"It was signed W. S. Churchill!"

"Winston Churchill?" I mulled the name over my tongue. Suddenly, my brain caught up, "You mean *the* Winston Churchill; the Prime Minister of England?"

"No, you silly girl, Lord Salisbury is the prime minister! Winston's father was in politics mind, but this man is just 24, same as me, but he *is* Sir Randolph Churchill's son!"
He looked down on me like the child I was, clearly not grasping the gravity of the news he was telling me.
"Mr. Logan's most prized guest," he continued, "He came and stayed here a few years back before he died."

My mind was racing how could Katie be secretly dating the world-famous Winston Churchill? The warm dry air of the Karoo blew through my hair. The horse under me straining against Edgar's tight reins. Suddenly, I realized how mindless I was being, of course Winston wasn't the Prime Minister of England…. Yet! He only took office in 1940, when he was 66! It was currently 1899!

"That's not even the worst of it!" said Edgar gleefully snapping me out of my heat induced day dream.

"There's more?" I asked turning my face upwards.

"Well it seemed the two rather hit it off. It would seem that Katie left, shall we say, a rather good impression on him!"

"Are they engaged?" I asked with the tone of an excited 10 year old.

"I don't know, but it would explain why she turned down young James last week. He has his sights on her to be his wife!"

"Never!" I protested, "She's only 17!"

"Exactly! She's been ready to marry for a year, well in polite circles most men would wait until she is 18, but she's so beautiful, funny, caring…"

I elbowed him in the guts to stop gushing. "If I didn't know any better, I'd say you have the same idea!" I teased.

"Maybe I do, or rather…" he paused his handsome face saddened at the thought, "Well maybe it's just not on the cards."

"So? Is that your big news then, that she may or may not be engaged to Winston?" my tone was that of disappointment. "Is that not juicy enough for you? A lowly girl in service potentially engaged to one of the grandest families in England?"

"I guess for *this time* that it is rather a sensation." I added.

"This time? Honestly Molly you speak as if you're from the future! Stop being so high and mighty!" he poked me back under my arms, tickling me. He was like the brother I had always wanted. I felt safe with him.
"But yes, it does get even more juicy!"

"Really?" I said, at once excited again.

"He was captured by the Boers!"

"What!"

"Yes, he was taken prisoner the day after Katie got here. His train, the one they both rode up in, continued onto the British Natal Colony, where the Boers derailed it by placing a large rock on the rails!"

"That's terrible!" I gasped. I had, until this point, built up a sympathy towards the Boers.

I had been trying to study the history of Southern Africa, in the vein hope that knowing more would give me a clue as to how to get back home to the future. I figured that I needed to find out the answer to my original question. *Why would my grandfather keep a bullet casing and a lump of lead for all these years?*

The Anglo-Boer war began, as all wars do, over resources. Diamonds and gold had been discovered in the Transvaal, but the tense relations between the Brits and the Boers stretched back to the late 18th Century, in 1795 when the British took control over the former Dutch colony in the Cape. The Boers refused to acknowledge the new governors and literally trekked* north. Relations however became even more strained when in 1833 the Emancipation act was brought in, freeing the local slaves and thus striking a huge blow to the Boer economy. They relied on free labour to run their farms.

Baba Zinzile's was apparently once part of the Xhosa royal family before his grandparents had been enslaved during the War of Nxele in 1817. The relationships between the Xhosa's and the British were also very tenuous as the so called *100 year war* between them had only recently ended. Their only common ground was their mutual hatred of the Boers. These ongoing battles over land ownership, resources and governance now once again rose to a head and again, many innocent lives put up as leverage for the benefit of an elite greedy few.

I looked from my mounted position, safe with Edgar on his horse, at the never-ending expanse of land. The hardy scrub bush smelt sweet as it sweated in the heat of the mid-afternoon sun. And in that moment, I could understand why people would fight over this. As a young girl, I could not understand the politics behind money but I could appreciate that longing to call the beauty, the rawness of the landscape, mine.

"Glorious isn't it!" said Edgar breaking the spell of silence as we ascended the last koppie* before rounding the final corner into town. "A little oasis in a mad world".

CHAPTER 6

December 1899

When Edgar had dropped me off at the front of the hotel I immediately ran up the turret to Katie's card room. She loved playing cards, and the games kept the wounded soldiers in good spirits, but I found her alone, slumped at her games table, sobbing. I should never have asked, but I did.

"What's wrong?"

I knew it must have been something to do with Winston but I couldn't let on that I knew anything, and that Edgar and I had spent the afternoon gossiping about their relationship.

"Don't play coy with me Molly!" Katie snapped as she stormed across the room towards the window, "I know you know so don't fain ignorance!"

Her words wasped at my checks and I flushed a deep red in embarrassment. The card room was used as a vantage point for the soldiers to scout the surrounding landscape for rogue

Boers wanting to launch an attack on the British headquarters set up in town. One could see for miles gazing out of the turret and I knew at once Katie must have seen me ride in with Edgar and put two and two together.

"We weren't talking about you," the lie leapt out of my mouth. Katie looked at me; her eyes fastened hard as if she wished her gaze could set me alight. The silence was palpable. I looked down at the floor like a child being caught in the act of stealing cookies. I relented under the pressure of her scrutiny.

"All I know is that some boy wrote to you and that his name is Winston Churchill, and that if he is the Winston Churchill I've heard of, he is very wealthy and his father was a respected guest here. Why is that a big deal?" I folded my arms defensively and slouched back on the cool stone wall of the small room.

"Why is it a big deal?" she bawled. Her eyes were wet with tears, "Because it's my life and everyone seems to be affecting MY life!"

"I'm sorry," I said unfastening my arms and reached out to her, offering a hug. She pushed me away.

"What is wrong with you?" I shouted, stung at the rejection.

"My love, my Winston, has been captured by the Boers! That is what is wrong!" she wrung her hands in dismay. "He is probably dead!" she sobbed into her lap like a little child in a crumpled heap.

"O he is not dead," I blurted out unthinking, fed up with her dramatic howling. Her eyes shot up from her crumpled position on the floor, wet with tears, her face poxed with red blotches from her salty tears. "What? Has news come of his release?" she gasped hopefully, now getting to her feet and beginning to calm down. I had to think quickly, I couldn't very well say her love was the next prime Minister of England, and I knew he couldn't be dead as I had come from the future!

"I have a feeling," I mumbled into my chest, unconfident in this most vague of answers.

As if sent by an angel, Edgar's face appeared at the door.
"He has escaped Katie!" Edgar beamed picking up on our not so private conversation.

"Who?"

"Winston! He has escaped from the Boers and is making his way down the Mozambican coast to rejoin the troops in the city of Ladysmith. I've just got the news now, it would seem the letter he originally wrote to you which you received this morning was kept in the same mail bag and was delayed by weeks! With this war everything is in disarray at the Post Office."

Katie dried her eyes and rushed across the room into Edgars arms. "You've just made me the happiest woman in the world!" she sighed into his large frame. But while she was comforted, you could see Edgars face fall. He knew then that he would never get to call Katie his, her heart truly belonged to someone else. His warm embrace stiffened as we heard footsteps coming up the turret stairs.

We all dispersed into opposite corners of the room as if we had been caught doing something wrong by a teacher. James, one of the deputies popped his head around the corner and strode into the room with a large bunch of wild flowers.

"You have company, I see," he commented looking down his nose at me and strode across the room rudely barging past Edgar and thrust the bouquet of flowers at Katie.

"These are for you," he said grinning like a mad man eyeing Katie up and down like some prize horse at a market.

Katie's tear stained face now flushed an even deeper scarlet than before. "It would seem I have delivered these just in time!" James remarked as he plucked the last tear rolling down Katie's face from her chin and wiped it on his military coat.

"Have these louts upset you?" he said turning to us, bristling.

"No," said Katie, trying to catch her breath and steady her emotions, "Just the opposite in fact." Her face beamed.

"Well why the tears then?" asked James. As if he had any right to enquire.

He was a deputy; but he had no business being here. The hotel was only for Generals or the wounded, and he was neither. His arrogance annoyed me and his overzealous confidence in the way he spoke to us girls made me feel uneasy.

"Tears of joy," said Katie as she placed the flowers on the games table. You could see she instantly regretted saying anything as she struggled to come up with a lie as to what had made her so happy. She knew now Winston was alive, but knew nothing of their future together. She couldn't risk it all now by blabbing about their romance like a silly school girl and get herself fired on the spot for indecency.

"Do tell. What is it that could possibly make you this happy?" James wasn't going to let his questions go unanswered and he glared at Edgar most menacingly.

"No need to be jealous James," sneered Edgar. He knew now James' fate was the same as his, to be cuckolded by the stunning Katie and cast off, for she only had eyes for Winston now. This thought of James suffering the same heart ache as him made him smile. Misery truly does like company, and this act of bravado by James would soon be slapped down.

"We were just discussing how we are to travel to Ladysmith," said Katie. Edgar and I looked at her our mouth wide open with surprise.

"We were?" I said under my breath looking up at Edgar who was now standing behind me. His hands on my shoulders like a protective cape.

"Katie, we had only begun talking about it," said Edgar his eyebrows flaring at her to explain where this was going, but following her lead uncertainly.

"Are you mad?" exclaimed James. "The siege has been ongoing for days now in Ladysmith, the Boers have the whole town surrounded! It's far too dangerous for you to go!"

"For once I'm in agreement with James," said Edgar stepping into the center of the room, "I was just now trying to convince her that it was a bad idea," said Edgar now adding to Katie's lie.

"Thus the tears?" James mused affectionately cupping Katie's face in his hand. "You don't like to be told what to do, do you?" he said rhetorically. "Sometimes my dear, you have to let us men do the thinking!" He slapped Edgar on the back solidly as if to be in mutual agreement. "Still," he continued in his belittling tone, "This doesn't explain why you are happy?"

"I'm happy to have a purpose," Katie's words muscled up to James' probing. "The troops are in desperate need of medical help." She was starting to sound more rational as the lie became more and more believable.

"You have plenty of purpose here," continued James.

"I think our care would be much appreciated at Intombi," Katie corrected. Determined now, that she was, in fact, going to Ladysmith.

"Our care?" queried James never missing a beat.
"Well I can't leave Molly here!" Katie exclaimed giving me a wicked wink. "I have to have another Lady to accompany

me, and, no offense Molly; I don't think your skills will be much missed here, for a short while anyway."

I gulped down a large mouthful of bile. I was about to be sick. I would have no hope of convincing anyone here to keep me on. My great-great grandparents who I had been living with for the past 3 months had no clue that I was their great-great granddaughter, to them I was Molly Orpen the orphan that Mr. Logan hired, and if he decided I was to help Katie, then that was it! What if I were sent to this war and died?

I had been talking to Chef just that morning about the battle in Ladysmith which had begun in November, and he had told me about the awful conditions. How some residents had fled the besieged town and were living in tented camps along the Klip River. How illness and disease was killing more people than the fighting was. The battle itself was ongoing but thankfully an agreement between an officer of the British army, Mr. White, and the leader of the Boers, Piet Joubert, was reached to allow the creation of a neutral Hospital called Intombi, some 5 kilometers outside the town of Ladysmith.

Intombi was the Zulu word for hippopotamus, so I could only assume that the local river was inhabited by these most ferocious of creatures! Indeed, I had been warned by Mary never to go to a river unescorted and to always look out for hippos at night when walking around, as they used the cool of the evening to walk vast distances to graze on fresh grass... not much of a worry in the middle of a desert here in Matjiesfontein, but Mary cautioned me to never assume anything in Africa, danger was always present.

The idea of having to fend off wild animals, to be in the center of a war, it was all too much for me to process, Edgar saw my face turn pale. "Katie you can't go! Look at poor Molly, you simply can't go!" he implored, but it was no good. Katie was determined to go to Winston; I was trapped by my lie, and caught in hers.

CHAPTER 7

February 1900

It had been a long two months since the funeral and the scandalous news of Katie's rumored romance, the memory of my peaceful ride into town with Edgar was now replaced with the true hellish realities of war. The smell of sweet grasses was exchanged with the stench of death and putrefying flesh. The pained screams of wounded men haunted every moment.

I wished now I had never ridden back into town with Edgar, in fact I wished I had never wished for anything, ever. If I had just done what my grandfather had asked and gone and fetched his books, if I had listened to my mother and not gone poking about where I shouldn't, I would be safe at home, probably lazing in front of the telly watching some brainless MTV cribs episode, or be paging through a tabloid magazine, studying the latest way to style your eyebrows.

There is that famous saying, 'be careful what you wish for'. I never wished for this. How could I have been so stupid…

It had taken Katie and me 3 weeks to get from Matjiesfontein to Ladysmith. We first caught the train from Matjiesfontein up towards Bloemfontein. This journey which usually took five days by train, took us eight, as the Boers had destroyed the railway bridges which crossed the Orange River at Norval's Pont and another at Bethulie.

The Boers' only hope at weakening their enemy was to destroy the railways which brought supplies and troops further inland, taking control out of the hands of the British. Baba Zinzile had been sent with us for protection. Mr. Logan, keen as ever to show his support for Queen and country, was thrilled with Katie's mad idea to journey up to the newly formed Intombi Hospital.

The journey was exhausting, like a bad dream. No sooner had we started, we were stopped. The locomotive driver was on constant look out for mines buried by the Boers under the railway tracks, along extensive stretches of rail where the train was meant to be going the fastest. The crude devices were made from a Martini Henry rifle, with a sawn off barrel and butt. The Boers converted live rounds into blanks by removing the bullets from the cartridges. The rifle was then loaded with this blank cartridge and then placed next to a dynamite percussion cap with the rifle barrel facing the cap and the trigger facing upwards. In this way the weight of a train going over the set up would trigger the rifle and dynamite. The effects were devastating and effective.

The only respite to this arduous journey towards, what I was sure would be my death, was the surrounding landscape. It was still dry but the scrub bush landscape of the Karoo had now turned to rough grasses of all shades of yellow and green. The tips of the longest grass shone, bleached by the sun, and rippled in the hot summer wind.

I kept thinking about what Edgar had said on the morning we left, "Fear is a tyrant and a despot Molly, more terrible than the rack, more potent than the snake." The thought of death, the fear of what was yet to come was probably the worst part about the journey. I suddenly realized why Katie had been so determined. She needed to know Winston was alright, she needed to know they would be together, not knowing would be worse than any reality.

Once we had disembarked from the train we were transferred onto a large train of wagons driven by oxen. The travel was slow. Baba Zinzile walked behind us, ever on the lookout for danger. At night we camped in a circle formation with a large fire in the center of the kraal* to fend off predators. Africa was still very wild, animals had free run, in contrast to a zoo, we were the attraction. On occasion we could hear the roars of a pride of lions in the distance and the chatter of jackals at sunset.

As we moved closer towards the Drakensburg Mountains the landscape changed again. The rich grassland now was peppered with Thorn trees which grew like large umbrellas. Their bark was like curled paper. There was a very specific type of tree we would look for to burn the locals called it ysterhout, or black ironwood, the trees had light grey bark and beautiful sweet smelling creamy white flowers. It was the best wood for fires as it burnt the longest. Baba Zinzile also said it was the finest wood to carve with, as it was so tough and long lasting.

Other parts of the journey were not so beautiful, vast tracks of veld* had been burnt under the scorched earth policy brought in by the British in response to the Boers wanton destruction of the railways and other essential services like cutting telegraph wires. Boers were driven out of their mountainous hiding spots like quail, in blocks. Blame was put on farm owners and locals near to where the destruction had occurred, suspected collusion with the Boers lead to houses in the vicinity of the damage being raised to the ground and residents made prisoners of war.

Innocent Afrikaaner women who were left by their husbands on their farms, alone, now had to flee the fires, many never escaped. Huge numbers of indigenous people, Zulus and Xhosa alike were driven from their homelands and forced into concentration camps. The whole country, and all who were in it were at war, and Katie and I were travelling towards the center of it all.

On our protracted passage through the steep mountains, across wide untamed rivers I had more of a chance to learn from Katie what Winston Churchill was like. He was a journalist by profession and a man driven to prove to his wealthy father that he was more than his title. He wanted to prove that he was a man within his own rights who could be someone. She showed me both the letters that Edgar had brought to her, that day of the funeral, detailing how Winston had been arrested and taken to Pretoria. The Boers knowing he was the son of a wealthy man planned to ransom him.

No sooner had Winston been imprisoned he plotted his escape. Disguised by wearing a vicar's hat he slipped under the floorboards in the room he was being held and managed to get outside. His next obstacle was a 10ft fence which he scaled. Finally, after breaking free his only option to get to safety was to follow the railway line in the direction of Delagoa Bay 300 miles away! Luckily, he managed to scramble onto a goods train where he hid under some coal sacks, eventually making it to a mining village where true to his luck he encountered the only British man around for miles who helped get him passage down the coast to Natal and onto Ladysmith. It was there that he wrote to Katie about the grueling journey and his valiant escape and his wish to see her again that kept him going.

It was so romantic almost too good to be true. Along with snippets of her loves great escape Katie also told me about our future hosts, Major General David Bruce and his wife Mary. They were going to meet us at Intombi and show us the ropes. Katie was not just eager to see Winston now, but also to help in her capacity as a nurse. After a miserable expedition, some days on foot, we arrived in Ladysmith.

CHAPTER 8

February 1900

The hospital was much bigger than I was expecting, it looked more like a tented village than a place of convalescence. The camp had been set up near to the Klip River with the main tent at the center holding 100 beds, all full. Each tent had a number assigned, and patients were separated by the nature of their injury and by race. In all there were around 215 medical workers including Katie and myself.

Across the railway, which separated the camp from the Military, were over 1000 civilians who were either helping at the hospital, or who had fled Ladysmith. At the onset of the battle the hospital seemed to cope, however as the siege continued the casualties built up to the point that there were no longer enough beds.

With over crowing came disease. The smell of the tented camp greeted us before we saw it. Typhoid and dysentery infected thousands of people and by the end of our stay more than 500 people had died from these diseases alone.

To make things worse was a severe lack of food. On the night we arrived and escorted into the nursing tents, we were served a dinner of gruel soup made from the boiled bones of some of the cavalry horses killed in battle.

The camp was as one would expect during a war, trenches dug around the tents for protection. It was hard work from dawn until dusk, and night shifts were not uncommon. Katie was ill tempered as when we arrived, Winston was nowhere to be found. After making some subtle enquires it would seem he was still on route, but nobody knew for sure where he was or if he was alive.

It was towards the end of my second week at Intombi that I was moved into a tent close to the Indian Field Hospital, the number of Indian casualties was immense. I had until this point not known about indentured labourers sent by their employers to fight. They were not slaves, but they were not free either. A man called Mohandas Gandhi was in charge; he had the friendliest of faces and smiled at me as I entered the tent.

"Good morning," he said whimsically as I pushed my way past two stretcher-bearers in the door way.

"Sorry," I nodded to the men at the door, "Good morning," I said rather sarcastically.

"You do not think it a good day?" he asked looking deep into my eyes. I brushed my hair out of my face, which was grubby and already beaded with sweat.

"No," I said tears pricking into my eyes, unexpectedly overcome with exhaustion and emotion. "No, to be honest it doesn't feel like a good day at all." A tear escaped and rolled down my chin.

"Then I think you better have another look around," he said gesturing to the room.

It was full to the rafters with men on beds, some on straw mats on the floor due to overcrowding; the room smelt of dried blood and sick. I looked at the faces of the men writhing in pain and then defiantly back at Mr. Gandhi.

"I see no good here," I spat.

He again looked deep into my eyes as if he were searching for something within me. "A 'No' uttered from the deepest conviction is better than a 'Yes' merely uttered to please, or worse, to avoid trouble." He said picking up fresh dressings and handing them to me, "at least you are honest."

I softened at his kind words, "Well what good do you see here then?"

"Each one of us has to find his peace from within. And for peace to be real, must be unaffected by outside circumstances. That is why today is good, as I have decided today to do good, and by that decision I feel good."

I smiled as I washed my hands in a small bowl of water on the table. "I suppose you are right in a way," I replied, " but I find it very hard to see the good in so much violence, and the suffering of so many."

"I object to violence because when it appears to do good, the good is only temporary; the evil it does is permanent." He agreed.

"My name is Molly," I smiled.

"It was good to meet you," he said picking up a stretcher and moved towards the door.

"What should I do here today? I was told you would instruct me." I said worried at being left alone to care for over 50 patients.

"Molly, you know what to do. Do good." He smiled as he picked up a stretcher and opened the flap of the tent allowing the warm sunlight to stream in. I must have looked confused. He smiled again, a heartfelt smile as if he had a secret knowledge of something and looked at me as if I could change the world.

"I will try to do my best," I grinned back relaxed in his confidence in my abilities.

"It's the action, not the fruit of the action, that's important. You have to do the right thing. It may not be in your power, may not be in your time, that there'll be any fruit. But that doesn't mean you stop doing the right thing. You may never know what results come from your action. But if you do nothing, there will be no result."

And with those wise words he dipped his head out of the tent and went off to collect fallen soldiers with his team of stretcher-bearers. Working in the harshest of conditions, endangering their own lives to save others, to do good.

I worked hard that day, harder than ever before and found the deepest sense of satisfaction when I collapsed into my stretcher bed that night next to Katie, that I had indeed done good. Just as I was about to close my eyes I noticed Katie get up and sneak towards the door. I could hear some muffled voices outside; a man's voice, familiar to me but too far away for me to recognise. I rolled over and told myself to mind my own business.

I slept deeply and when I was woken up by the matron I felt refreshed and re-inspired, finally at peace with my fate, I was stuck back in time and maybe I would never go home, but I must have been sent back for a reason, maybe that reason was to help.

"Today is a good day," I said quietly to myself as I put on my white apron covered in brown blood stains.

"Molly," came a stern voice from behind me. It was Mary Bruce. She was the head nurse; her husband had been the one to broker the agreement with general Joubert to form Intombi.

"Yes Maam," I jumped up and bowed my head looking at my shoes respectfully.

"Where is your friend Katie? She was meant to meet my husband early this morning. A friend of hers has arrived."

So that's what I must have heard last night, a secret tryst between Katie and Winston, he must have arrived early and surprised her!

But where was she now? It was not like her to be away this long, come to think of it, I couldn't recall if she had even come back to bed last night.

"I haven't seen her," I said unhelpfully to Mrs. Bruce. Mrs. Bruce turned and strode off out of the tent irritably; she was too busy to have to go on a hunt for Katie.

I got up and laced up my small leather boots, a parting gift from Edgar, and made my way to the mess hall for breakfast. She must be there I thought. How pleased she would be to know Winston was here, if she didn't know already.

I was just rounding the corner past the last tent when I saw a mass of people gathered around in a circle, some shouting some women were crying around a body.

"What's going on?" I demanded and pushed my way into the crowd.

There in the mud, lay my best friend in the entire world. Katie.

Her beautiful hair, wet and matted into the ground, a gaping wound at her temple. It looked as if her head had been struck heavily with a rock. Her dress was pulled up around her waist and her legs were cut and bruised. I ran forward and collapsed at her side.

"Get a doctor!" I screamed like a child.

"Someone get help! Don't just stand there!" I yelled at the sea of faces that looked down on me pitifully.

A hand was placed on my shoulder. "It's no good Molly, she's gone." Said a familiar voice, the same voice I had heard last night.

It was James.

No sooner had he touched me I knew everything. He was the one who had to have done this. He couldn't stand the rejection. He couldn't bare that Katie loved someone else who would rather be in a war zone, than near to him.

"YOU DID THIS!" I bellowed as I got up to my feet, my fists clenched, and landed a solid blow to his gut. "You did this! Didn't you!" I demanded hysterically; hitting him ever harder. He wrapped his arms around me as if to hug me, and restrained my arms. He lifted me off the ground and whispered chillingly into my ear.
"Shut-up Molly! Or you will meet the same fate."

I spat in his face and he dropped me.

"She is in shock. Doctor you need to sedate her she is hysterical." James said to the gathering crowd and waved over a large man with a glass syringe filled with morphine. I tried to get away but James held me down. My face pressed into the mud next to Katie's. I looked at her beautiful face. She had her whole life in front of her. She was in love. This was, this was ....the morphine raced through me and I was out.

I woke up in the dark my head throbbing; I opened my eyes praying that it had all been a dream. Everyone around me was asleep. The camp was eerily silent. James was sitting in a chair at the foot of the bed his head resting to one side. On his lap his pistol was drawn. I breathed in deeply, the nightmare was real. The smell of rain was in the air and there was an ominous feeling about the room I was in. I slowly sat up desperate not to wake the murderer who had been left to 'guard me'. I could kill him so easily. I thought to myself. I could snatch his pistol, point it at his chest and blow him away.

The thought was relished in my mind, then curdled with sour bitterness; I wanted him to suffer more. An easy death was too good for him. The Boers were famed for using poisoned bullets which worsened the infection of British soldier's wounds. If I could make him feel pain forever I mused. As quietly as I could, I tiptoed out of the bed and lifted the weapon from his lap. I raised it up and was just about to pull the trigger when I saw the glow of a candle at the far end of the tent.

My arms felt bruised from where I had been held down. The tender bump on my arm where the doctor had injected me throbbed as my pulse raced.
"Who's there?" I whispered towards the light, the weapon trembling in my hands. James shifted, but didn't wake. The light came closer and closer, it was floating towards me; the figure behind it cloaked in darkness.

"Hello Molly," It was Mr. Gandhi. "Come with me." His voice was warm and comforting. "Come with me Miss Molly," he said again, now taking the pistol out of my clammy hands and removed the bullets from the barrel. He placed the small lumps of lead into the palm of my hand and placed the weapon on the table next to James' sleeping head. "Come now," this time he sounded more urgent. I reached my other hand out to his and he led me out of the tent.

"It's not fair!" I sobbed as he led me outside. The air was damp and you could hear jackals barking in the distance, scavenging the campsite. "You should have let me kill him! An eye for an eye!" I yelled. He smiled and patted my head solidly.

"Miss Molly, an eye for an eye only ends up making the whole world blind."

Near the mess hall was a cart loaded with supplies and Baba Zinzile was yoking up the cattle. I looked back at the camp site my heart heavy, thudding in my chest.

"It's not fair," I said to him.

"What isn't fair?" questioned Gandhi.

"That you let him live, he killed my best friend. I know it!" I said with conviction.

"Ah," he sighed as he lifted me carefully into the back of the wagon. "What makes her life more important than theirs?" he gestured towards the large grave pits that had been dug to accommodate the sheer number of casualties. "This war has seen enough death; you do not need to take a life to feel justice. There is a higher court than courts of justice and that is the court of conscience. It supersedes all other courts. Keep these as a symbol of this lesson."

He pressed my fist holding the bullets towards the center of my chest. I could feel my heart beating strongly. I was so angry yet so sad at the same time; so exhausted to have come all this way and to have lost everything. I clambered into the far corner of the wagon and prepared for the long journey back to Matjiesfontein.

CHAPTER 9

28th February 1900

A few days after I had left Ladysmith news came to us on the road that the siege was over. Buller and his men had persevered against all odds and that Winston had come into town just a day after I had left. Tragically, he would never know that Katie had travelled across the country to see him. He would never know how much she loved him. He would never know that the controlling jealousy of another man robbed him of a potential future of much happiness. I wondered how things would have changed in the course of history had Katie lived. Would Winston and her have married and stayed in South Africa and raised a family, or was he always destined to become Prime Minister of England one day?

We stopped over at a small holding for the night near Aliwal. The farm owner's wife arranged for me to have a warm bath in her room and was kind enough to brush my hair which hadn't smelt this lovely in months. The maids brought in buckets of warm water which had been heated over a fire outside in the back courtyard. The water was scalding hot as it was poured over my back as I sat in the large steel bath. The stripping heat felt somewhat cathartic as I focused my mind on the warmth as it flowed over me entirely.

I tried to smile at my host's kindness, but it seemed disloyal to smile so easily at the smell of clean hair when my best friend was dead and cold in the ground.

"War is not easy," she offered; sensing my awkwardness.

"I'm sorry, you have been so kind. It's just that I lost my friend." I said as I got out of the bath tub and got into a pretty old dress the kind lady had laid out for me.

"She is not lost," the lady smiled, "She is here, in your heart where you will keep her always." Her thick Afrikaans accent was comforting and reminded me of my mother.

I blinked back the tears. My host offered me a cotton handkerchief with a beautiful embroidered buttercup. Her initials were sewn in; M.O.

I looked up, "You have the same initials as me!" I offered finally able to speak through the tears.

"Then it a sign that it must be yours," she said smiling.

"Thank you." I said and tucked the precious gift up my sleeve for safe keeping.

That night I didn't sleep word had come of rogue Boers in the mountains and we were advised to move on after dinner. We trundled through the sweet smelling veld. The road here was long and flat and Baba Zinzile lead the way with lit torches of fire that smoldered in the night air. I felt in my pocket and found the tiny lumps of lead Mr. Gandhi had given me. I wrapped the bullets in the handkerchief and stuffed them into my pocket. The moon glittered in the sky like a large silver coin, watching us wind our way into the next town of Graaf Reinet.

I watched the sun come up and set over the week long journey and it felt as if the warm rays were now different on my skin. I was no longer that young sensitive girl that had come, transported by fairies, to this world, but a hardened girl who felt that hoping and dreaming were now childhood memories. I felt empty and alone, I felt that all the happiness had been drained from the world, in stark contrast to where I stood, in the most beautiful place on Earth, looking over the bowl of the Great Karoo.

"The locals call this The Valley of Desolation," came a soft voice from behind me. I looked around, my eyes like hardened steel. I had run out of tears. A short lady, about my height walked towards me. Her thick brown hair tied back.
"You must be headed to Maitjiesfontein," she mused as she sat on a rocky boulder and plucked a long stalk of grass form a thicket besides her. She patted the large tanned stone and gestured for me to sit.

"Come far?" she offered again. I wandered over, my leather shoes worn and battered by the long journey, felt thin under my feet. I sat down besides the lady with a heavy thud.

"I've often wondered why and how the Christians came to invent Hell." She began, "But last night when I was lying in bed it struck me that the early Christians lived in a time very much like this under the Roman Empire during its decline and fall; and of course the poor things believed in Hell because they saw it." She took my hand in hers like my mother would when I was scared during a storm, and just held it.

"You are not alone," she said instinctively.

"I feel alone," I said finally to this stranger; gazing into the distance while the cattle grazed behind us, champing hungrily at the new stems of grass.

"You must tell Mr. Logan that I send my regards, and give my best to his wife." She squeezed my hand reassuringly.

I smiled finally, "You know the Logan's?"

"Yes, quite well, in fact, at one time we were neighbors. I lived in the cottage next to the post office in town."

"You must be Olive Shreigner!" I exclaimed, excited to have remembered the infamous resident. "Edgar Wallace now lives in your house!" I chimed.

"Ah," she said releasing my hand and popping it firmly in my lap.

"He is a writer like you! He told me all about you! About your tree on the hill and about your views on the war," I paused, suddenly remembering more.

"Go on," she smiled daringly. "What about my views on the war?"

"That, well, that you had a disagreement with one of Mr. Logan's guests about the Boers," my head sunk down again. The first real friendly conversation I'd had in weeks and I had just blown it by confessing to idle gossip.

She rolled her head back and laughed loudly. "I'm glad they are still talking about it, must mean I hit a nerve."

"Are you coming back into town with us?" I asked hoping I'd have a friendly face around the hotel, now that Katie was gone.

"No, unfortunately I'm needed elsewhere," she said simply, "we just happen to be crossing the same path and you looked so sad, and well, us women need to look out for each other! We are not the ones at war; it's the greed of men that has lead us to where we are now. You on one side, me on the other, silly when we sit here chatting as friends."

I got to my feet and dusted myself off. "We are not on different sides, I just don't have a choice," I said gesturing to the group of British soldiers I was travelling with.

"We all have a choice. We always have a choice, if not a duty to be true to our own hearts. If you were to choose, who's side would you be on?"

"I wouldn't pick a side," I said finally after considering the question for a long time looking at the ancient landscape in front of me, time worn by the desert winds. I couldn't imagine this place, so dry so desolate once being an inland sea, teaming with life under its waters.

"Why do you say that? Do you feel the Boers are wrong to fight against the British?"

"No, I just feel that it is having to choose a side which divides us. Men vs women, countries against each other. Constantly, us versus them. It's exhausting, it's unnecessary. Why can't we just share the world? Why does one thing have to belong to someone? Like this view," I said gesturing over the vast expanse of wilderness, stretched out in front of us as far as the eye could see. "It is no more yours than it is mine, yet we fight over the land? Animals seem to have a natural order, the crocodiles in the rivers, the hippos on the banks, the lions in the grasses and the leopards in the mountains, the birds in the trees and sky, why can't we just accept our differences and just live together as people?"

"You have the innocence of a child," Olive said as she took my hand and lead me back to the cart which Baba Zinzile was getting ready. Yoking up the fat cattle.

"I am a child," I smiled back at her, "I'm only 10."

"Well for someone who is only 10 you have the wisdom of someone much older, you remind me of a girl called Lyndall," she said.

"117 years older perhaps," I joked to myself as I hopped into the cart. It lurched away, the final stretch of our journey, nearly over. Olive waved us off as the troop of us descended the steep mountain pass into the heart of the Karoo.

CHAPTER 10

March 1900

"Bang!" the shot rang out in the cold morning air, waking me from my deep sleep. I scrambled out of bed and ran into Stella's room. The air was thick with smoke. I could hear Jesse, crying from his Cot at the foot of my bed...

And here I was. A ten year old girl. A girl who had travelled through time, traversed the southern part of Africa, now fleeing again to somewhere new.

I remember the desperate faces of Stella and Rudi as they hurried Jesse and me onto the train to Cape Town. Their home on fire but their most precious asset, Jesse, safe with me... This was the first time since I arrived that it had been just me, in charge of my own fate. No fairy to save me, no kind friend, no wise man to protect me from my inner demons, just Jesse and me.

When the conductor, William Coal, came over I felt so grateful that I had someone who I could unburden myself to. Someone who was just there to listen, he didn't have to understand. I needed someone to know the real me, I could keep the pretense up no longer. I was tired to my bones, and for the first time truly, truly, I wanted nothing more than to be home with family my loving mother, my irritating sister, my dad; my normal life.

Jesse wriggled on my lap uncomfortably as I felt something digging into my hip. His fat little body like a sack of potatoes on my skinny legs. I dug my hand deep into my pocket to remove the poking lump.

I pulled out a beautiful handkerchief with a beautifully embroidered buttercup with my initials M.O stitched in. I had forgotten all about them, I thought them lost during my travels back to Maitjiesfontein. Delicately, I unwrapped the parcel remembering the bullets Mr. Gandhi had given to me. All at once it struck me. The items that teleported me here, the little lumps of lead the bullet casing; they were not my great grandfathers, they were not my grandfathers, they were mine! I was the one to keep them all this time, I was the answer to my own question!

But if I had them in the future, that must have meant that I could go there again, a loop. Without the bullets I would never had made the wish, without the wish I would never have adventured on to find them. So which came first?

The train lurched to a standstill and Mr. Coal ambled up the train towards me. My mind was racing I felt like I nearly had the answer.

"Time to go," he said ominously.

"What do you mean?" I said confused.

"To the post office, I have someone there who will take you in for the night," he smiled kindly, "Are you feeling any better?"

he felt my forehead like a worried parent does when one is sick.

"I just want Jesse to be safe," I said with all the strength I could muster. "My only wish is that he gets to this address," I pulled out a scrap of paper with an address in Tokei Stella had put in the wicker basket, "And that he be safe and well."

I closed my eyes to steady myself for the next part of the journey but when I opened them I found myself back in the study! Back in my grandfather's cool, damp, musty study! I was home!

I hadn't a moment to adjust to what had just happened when I saw the handle of the great mahogany door turning to open. Instinctively, I hid in the footwell of the large writing desk, not knowing what time I was in, or who exactly would be coming through the door.

In my hands I no longer held a scrappy piece of paper or a little boy, I held the crumpled handkerchief and bullets.
I peeked up from my hiding place hoping to see my mother or sister, but instead, I saw myself... I was gathering books and poking about.

So rude and nosey, I thought as I looked at myself. She walked towards me. I crept further into the cover of darkness under the desk. Tucked between the wall and the back of the footwell was an old first aid tin which must have slipped down here years ago. I fished it out of the crevice. I carefully placed the bullets and handkerchief inside it for safe keeping. I didn't want to lose them again! Just to be sure I scratched my initials into the enamel paint on the front.

The other me was still poking about, so lazy, I thought watching myself stroll around the room gathering books gazing at the wall, Have you not got chores to do? I thought angrily looking at the brat I was. My legs started to cramp up. What was I going to do, I was trapped here in my hiding place, what would happen if that me saw me?

Just as I was building up the courage to confront myself when the other me went out of the door onto the landing. I got up out of the footwell.

"Hello!" came a twinkling voice from the desk. I swung around and glared at the menacing fairy who sat nonchalantly on the corner of the desk.

"Hello! Hello? Is that what you have to say!" I flew into a rage and grabbed the fairy in both hands, dropping the precious tin and its contents onto the floor.

She disappeared in a puff of smoke and reappeared on the picture frame of the old farm house. "Took you long enough," she jibed as I tore across the room towards the wall of pictures
.

"I went through hell!" I yelled not caring now who heard me. "You left me in hell!" my face was puce with rage.

"You are the one who wished for it!" she said flitting onto my shoulder as if she hadn't a care in the world that I might just swat her to death like a fly.

"I wished to know why my grandfather kept these items, with my initials! You could have told me it was me all along!"

"I couldn't very well do that!" she retorted playing with my silky red hair. "You wouldn't have believed me, also if I had told you, you might never have gone back in time in the first place, trapping yourself there forever, so you see I had to let you do it, as you did it before, as you are about to do now…"
She flittered over to the door, the other me pushed the door open and strode across the room, as if I wasn't there are

marched right through me, and picked up the tin I had dropped on the floor.

"What's going on?" I said to the fairy anxiously. Was I dead? She placed a finger over her thin lips as I watched my other self fatefully pick up the tin and ask that vital question, "I wish I knew why…."

In a pillar of light my doppelganger was gone.

"You will get used to it," said the fairy returning to my shoulder as if we were age old friends.

"I'm never wishing for anything ever again!"

"We'll see," she said ominously and vanished.

"Molly!" came a shrill but familiar voice from the hallway behind me, "come down stairs at once, and look at the mess you left here!"

"Mum!" I shouted and ran out of the dusty old study like a dog out of the gates. I tore down the carpeted stairs and raced past the TV, I barreled into the kitchen to see my mom, my beautiful mom with a face of thunder glaring at me.

I ran straight into her arms hugged her and began to cry. "I missed you so much mummy!" I howled into her warm sweet smelling knitted jumper.

"Whatever is the matter with you?" she said holding me back at arm's length. "What's with all these tears? You've only been upstairs for 20 minutes! O darling," she said brining me in for a bear hug, "I'm not angry about the mess, it's just you know Grampa Jesse is living down stairs now so we need to keep everything neat and tidy. Stop crying now child"

"Grampa Jesse!" I yelped, my heart giving a leap. I had been holding his father just moments ago, my wish must have come true. Mr. Coal must have taken the baby boy to Tokei as I had wished.

"Where is he?" I demanded.

"Where do you think he is dear?" mom said shaking her head. "He is having a nap in his new room, but you can go and wake him for tea. It's getting late and I don't want him stalking around the house like he does in the middle of the night when he can't sleep, crashing into things."

I did not need to be told twice. I skidded down the passageway and launched myself into his room. It smelt like fresh paint and new carpet. I crept up to his bedside and stroked his head. He opened his big blue eyes, like his fathers.

"Molly" he said rather startled by his grandchild cooing over him.

"Grampa! You have fairies in your house and I met your father! "I began. He chuckled and sat up in his bed.

"Fairies hey," he said indulgently. "Tell me more of this encounter."

And so I did, I told him everything, from start to finish. He said I had quiet an imagination and that I should write it all down. So here I am, writing it all down. My journey through everlasting time!

A Journey Through Everlasting Time

ABOUT THE AUTHOR

Harriet E.F Clay (n Knight) was born in South Africa on September 3, 1987. After 12 years at the beautiful St Mary's D.S.G in Pretoria, she attended Rhodes University where she qualified as a radio journalist and teacher.

In 2012 she moved to the UK and began teaching in earnest and found the rich diversity London offered, wonderful inspiration for her books.

You can find Harriet prowling around The National Portrait Gallery on weekends and during the week she teaches. The children in her class are her biggest assets, constantly giving her ideas for her books and motivating her to finish them!

Harriet did not always think she would become an author, she had visions of being an artist, having won the Currie Van Schalkwyk art prize in 2003,2004 and again in 2005. She had her first group exhibition at the Sandton Civic Art Gallery when she was 17.

Most of her books are illustrated by her, however, in this book her mother Jane Knight was the creative spark.

Harriet has said before that most of the credit must go to her pupils who have listened tirelessly to each chapter as her books are written and provide invaluable feedback.

About the Characters in the book

Winston Churchill

Winston really was a reporter during the Boer war and really was captured by the Boers and held as a prisoner in Pretoria before his daring escape. Whether he actually met a girl called Katie and had a secret romance during his time there we will never know. But he did find happiness when he returned to London and met Clementine Ogilvy Hozier at a dinner party in 1908 and went on to have a rich and full life with her.

Mahatma Gandhi

Many people don't know that Gandhi was involved in the relief of Ladysmith during The Boer War in Southern Africa. Gandhi was a lawyer working for Muslim Indian Traders in Natal when he formed a volunteer Ambulance Corps for the British Army. People around the world revere Gandhi for the messages of peace he preached to the world and he is most well-known for his dedication towards human rights for Indians living in India during the formation of Pakistan. Sadly he was assassinated in 1948.

General Haig

Field Marshall Douglas Haig is most associated with the Battle of the Somme in World War One but was also part of the Anglo Boer war where he saw action alongside the 17th Lancers. You can learn more about him if you visit Edinburgh Castle where there is a bronze statue of him, mounted on his horse in the main courtyard outside the War Museum.

James Logan

James Logan took Matjiesfontein, which was originally only a small depot and farm along the railway, and expanded it into a vibrant Victorian village when he bought land there. Mr. Logan is remembered for his successful entrepreneurial spirit which took him from working on the railways into investigating corruption which led to the fall of the first government of Prime Minister Cecil Rhodes in 1893.

General Wauchope

Was a British Army officer, who died at the Battle of Magersfontein, he was rumoured to be a good friend of James Logan, he was as this story tells, buried twice!

Edgar Wallace

Edgar Wallace was a prolific writer who is most well-known for his creation of King Kong. He was, in his early years, a war correspondent, first for Reuters and then the Daily Mail in Matjiesfontein. He did find happiness (not with Katie) and wed Ivy Maude Caldecott and returned to London in 1903 where he went on to write a great many books, specifically mystery stories.

Nurse Katie

Nurse Katie was a real nurse during The Boer War and assisted in Matjiesfontein. Rumour has it that her ghost still haunts the Lord Milner Hotel, after dying at the age of 19 under dubious circumstances. Katie was renowned for playing cards with the patients in residence at the hotel during the war. You can even visit her room if you visit Matjiesfontein and listen for the tell-tell sounds of her ghost shuffling a pack of cards.

Olive Shreigner

May just be one of the most well-known residents of Matjiesfontein, at least to many South African's or literary scholars, for her tale, The Story of an African Farm. Olive was staunchly anti-war, and but rather campaigned strongly for the rights of Jews, Indians and the Boers.

Harriet Clay

Made in the USA
San Bernardino, CA
09 April 2017